P9-DNM-529

The Donkey's Christmas Song

written and illustrated by

NANCY TAFURI

Scholastic Press   New York

Copyright © 2002 by Nancy Tafuri

All rights reserved. Published by Scholastic Press, a division of Scholastic Inc., *Publishers since 1920.*

SCHOLASTIC, SCHOLASTIC PRESS, and associated logos are trademarks and/or registered trademarks of Scholastic Inc.

No part of this publication may be reproduced, or stored in a retrieval system, or transmitted in any form or by any means, electronic,

mechanical, photocopying, recording, or otherwise, without written permission of the publisher. For information regarding

permission, write to Scholastic Inc., Attention: Permissions Department, 557 Broadway, New York, NY 10012.

LIBRARY OF CONGRESS CATALOGING-IN-PUBLICATION DATA

Tafuri, Nancy.

The donkey's Christmas song / by Nancy Tafuri.   p. cm.

Summary: Various animals welcome a new baby born in a stable with their special sounds,

but the donkey is afraid that his braying will be too harsh.   ISBN 0-439-27313-7

[1. Animals—Fiction. 2. Jesus Christ—Nativity—Fiction. 3. Christmas—Fiction.] I. Title.

PZ7.T117 Don 2002   [E]—dc21   2001057655

10 9 8 7 6 5 4 3 2 1   02 03 04 05 06   Printed in Mexico 49   First edition, October 2002

The illustrations were painted in watercolors, pencils, and inks. The text was set in 36-point Calligraph 421.

Title type and author's name were hand-lettered by David Coulson.

Book design by Nancy Tafuri and David Saylor

*To Cristina
and to all
a song of peace*

Under a bright star,
a long, long time ago…

a baby was born
in a stable.

The animals wanted to
welcome the baby
with their song.

But the shy little donkey
was afraid his bray
was too loud.

So, the first to welcome the baby
were the doves.
Cooo, cooo,
they sang their slow, sweet song.

Then the cow
welcomed the baby.
Mooo, mooo,
she sang her low, warm song.

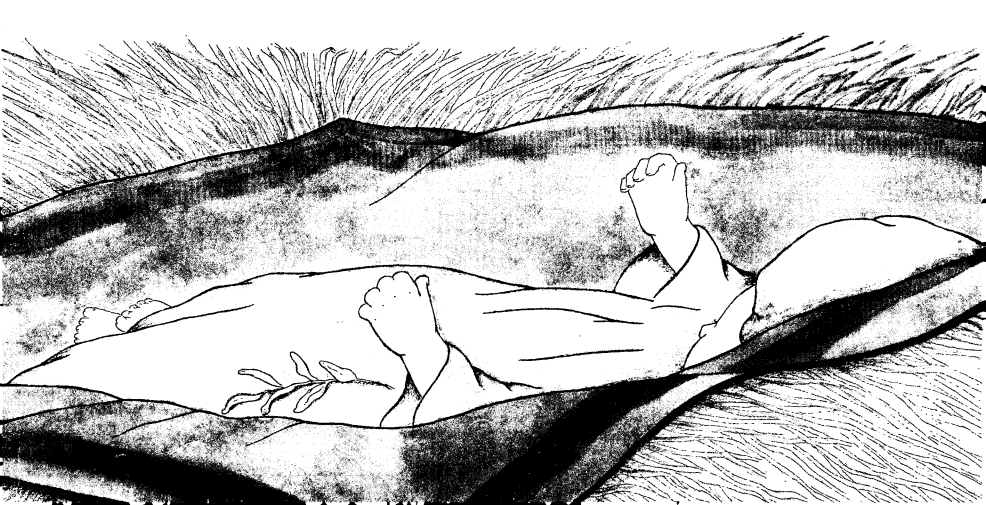

Then the goats
welcomed the baby.
Maaa, maaa,
they sang their gentle song.

Then the sheep
welcomed the baby.
Baaa, baaa,
they sang their tender song.

And the chicks
welcomed the baby.
Cheep, cheep,
they sang their little song.

And the mice
welcomed the baby.
Eeep, eeep,
they sang their quiet song.

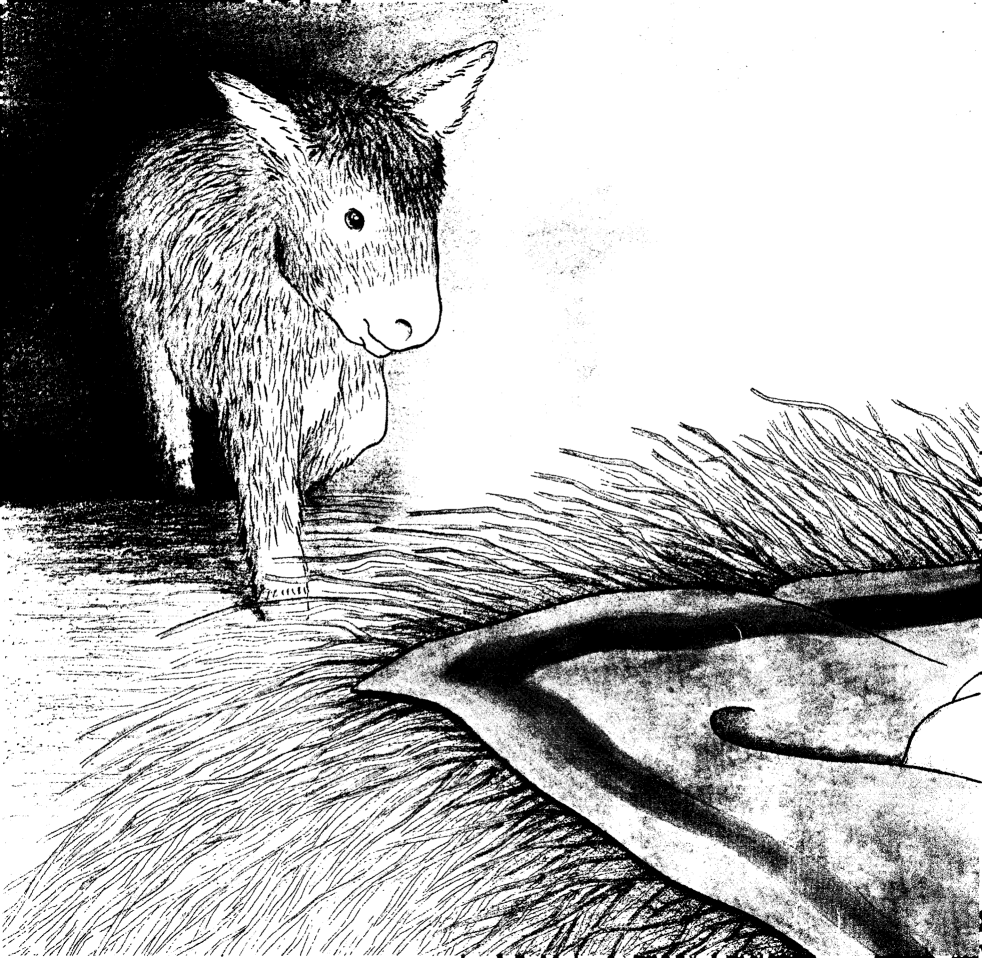

Then the baby looked over
at the shy little donkey.
The baby welcomed the donkey
with his smile.

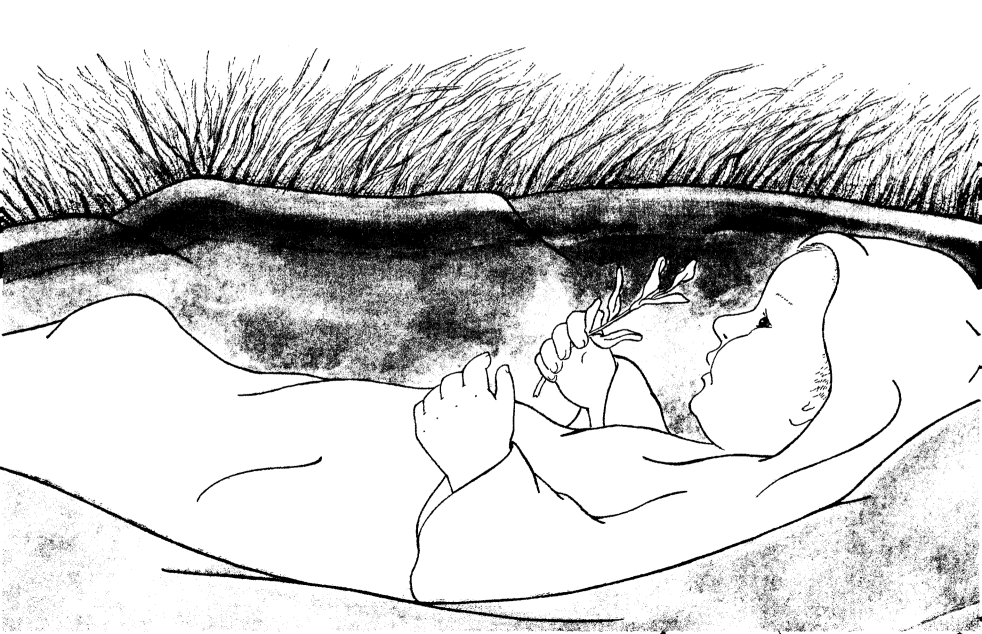

The donkey sang his noisy song.
Hee-aw! Hee-aw! Hee-aw! . . .

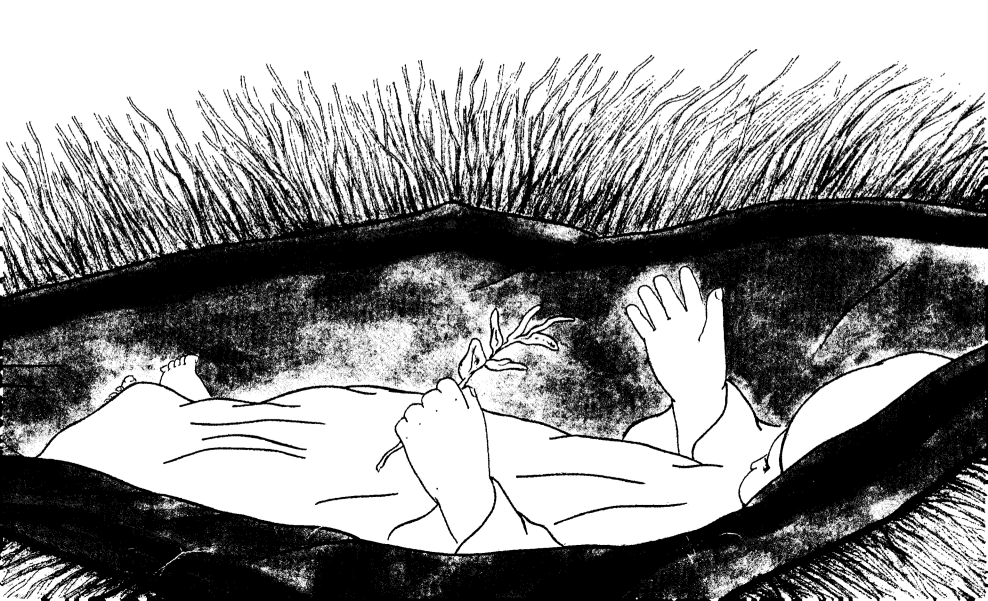

and the baby laughed with joy!

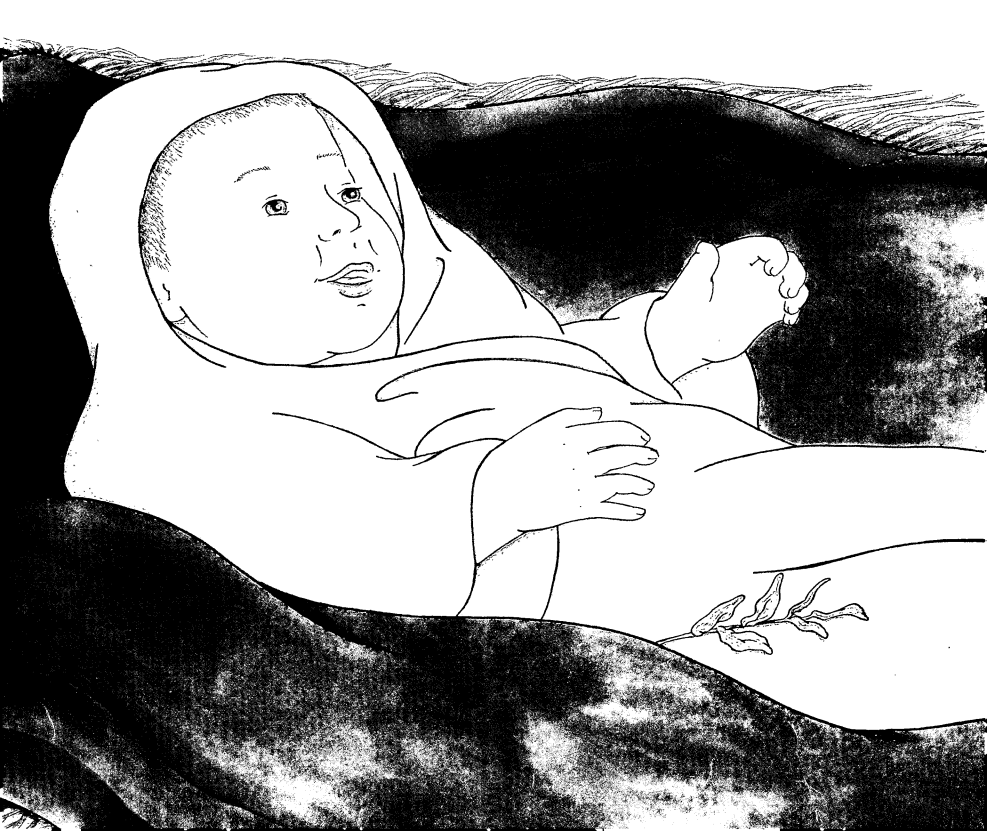

Then the donkey
snuggled close. . .

and kept the baby warm. . .

under that bright star
a long, long time ago.